This Book Belongs To:

Beth Ann Taylor

The Muppet Babies live in a nursery
in a house on a street that is a lot like yours.
But they can travel anywhere anytime using a special power—
the power of the imagination.
Can you imagine what it would be like to go with them?
Join the Muppet Babies on this adventure and find out.

Weekly Reader Presents

A Love Note for Baby Piggy

By James Howe • Illustrated by Kathy Spahr

Muppet Press/Marvel

Weekly Reader Books offers several exciting
card and activity programs. For information,
write to WEEKLY READER BOOKS, P.O. Box 16636,
Columbus, Ohio 43216.

This book is a presentation of
Weekly Reader Books.

Weekly Reader Books offers book clubs for children
from preschool through high school.

For further information write to:
Weekly Reader Books
4343 Equity Drive
Columbus. Ohio 43228

Weekly Reader is a trademark of Field Publications.

ISBN 0-87135-098-X

Printed in the United States of America

One sunny morning, Baby Piggy woke early. "What a great day!" she thought, rubbing the sleep from her eyes. She gazed at Baby Kermit, who was still sleeping, and sighed. "What a great frog!"

Just then, she noticed something sticking out from under her pillow. She pulled out a large sheet of paper with writing on it. All around the writing was a heart made of bits of yarn and buttons and used erasers and pieces of an old banana peel and all sorts of interesting things.

"What does this mean?" Baby Piggy wondered. "Someone has sent me a note. And this writing...why, it must be a secret code!"

Piggy looked at Kermit and sighed once again. "I'll bet it's a love note from Kermit. I'll imagine what it says. I know the kinds of things he would say to me if only he were brave enough."

Baby Piggy imagined the note to say:

I love you, Piggy, it's plain to see.
Please, oh please, will you marry me?

"Marriage?" Piggy thought. "I'm so young! But, yes, Kermie, I will marry you." She imagined herself walking down the aisle to the tune of "Here Comes the Pig."

All their friends were at the wedding. Everyone was having fun.

"I could dance all night," Piggy said as Kermit swept her across the floor.

"You're as light as a marshmallow," said Kermit, "and twice as sweet. But we must leave."

"Leave? We didn't eat yet."

"I know," said Kermit, "but it's time for us to go on our honeymoon."

Baby Piggy looked at the love note again and
imagined it to say:

A bright blue balloon, with streamers unfurled,
will take us away on a trip 'round the world.

"Will it take us to Paris, France?" Baby Piggy asked
Kermit. "I've always wanted to go there."
"Then Paris it is, my little gumdrop," Kermit replied.
And off on the breeze they flew.

"Oh, look," cried Piggy. "There's the Awful Tower. I don't see what's so awful about it."

"Uh, Piggy," said Kermit, "I think it's called the Eiffel Tower."

"Never mind," replied Piggy. "Now that we're here, when do we eat? I hear the French fries are out of this world."

"Not yet," said Kermit. "I have a surprise for you first."

Kermit took Piggy to a fancy shop.
"A Paris party dress!" said Piggy as she looked at
her presents. "And matching socks!"

"Gee," she thought, "Kermie gives me the nicest things." Then she said aloud, "Now, how about something to eat?"

But Baby Kermit just grabbed her hand and whisked her off to the waiting balloon. Soon they were flying over the tops of huge trees and vines. "The jungle?" Piggy gasped.

"Yes, my little potato chip," said Kermit. "We're going on a safari. Isn't that romantic?"

"I...I guess so. As long as the animals aren't as hungry as I am."

On top of their elephant, Piggy and Kermit rode through the leafy jungle. They saw tigers and monkeys and strange birds of many different colors. Crossing a river, they were surrounded by crocodiles with open mouths.

"I wish we were someplace else," Piggy whimpered,
hugging brave Baby Kermit. Then she thought, "I know
a way out of this!" Piggy imagined that the note also said:

Tell me your wish, from the most to the least,
I'll take you away, North, South, West, or East!

This time, the balloon carried them to China.
"These gardens are so-o-o beautiful," Baby Piggy
sighed after the balloon had landed.

"Not half as beautiful as you, my little fortune cookie," said Kermit.

"I wish you'd stop mentioning food," said Piggy. "I'm starved! Oh, look, there's a place to eat. Let's go!"

Inside the restaurant, Piggy said, "I can't decide whether to have the chop-suey burger or the pizza with noodles."

Just then, the waiter appeared. Piggy looked at him for a long time. For some reason, she felt as if she knew him.

"I brought you my favorite dish," said the waiter. "It's rubber bands and mud balls, lightly fried in a delicate moss sauce."

Now Piggy was sure she knew the waiter. "Gonzo!" she shouted. "What are you doing here? This is *my* fantasy!"

"Well, what do you think of the dish?" Gonzo asked. "Do you like it?"

Suddenly Baby Piggy felt someone poking her in the ribs. It was Gonzo. She was back in the nursery. Nanny had already brought in breakfast.

"Do you like it?" Gonzo asked again.

"Like what?" said Piggy.

"My note," said Gonzo. "I made it all by myself."
"This note is from you?"
Gonzo nodded.
"I should have known," said Piggy. She tried to hide her disappointment.

Piggy marched over to Kermit, who was standing by the breakfast table. "Kermie," she said, "I can't believe this love note isn't from you." She wiped away a tear. "After all, you called me your little marshmallow, your little gumdrop, your little fortune cookie, even your little potato chip!"

"Gee," said Kermit, shaking his head. "I don't know what you're talking about. But you sure sound hungry. Why don't you eat breakfast?"

Baby Piggy sat down at the breakfast table and began to eat. "There's nothing like a little cinnamon toast, jam, oatmeal, scrambled eggs, orange juice, and a banana to make you feel better," she said with a sigh.

As they were eating, Kermit leaned over and said,
"Piggy, will you—"
   "Yes?" Piggy asked eagerly.
   "Will you play with me after breakfast?"

Baby Piggy smiled sweetly. "Of course I will, my little...my little...Kermie. Let's pretend we're going on a trip around the world in a big blue balloon."

"Okay," said Kermit.

And that's exactly what they did.